Mother,

How little I knew;
How brilliant you are.

- Shanalee

Corinthians 13:11

www.mascotbooks.com

My Mama Loves Me: I'm Her Little Girl

For more information, please contact:
Mascot Books
560 Herndon Parkway #120
Herndon, VA 20170
info@mascotbooks.com

Library of Congress Control Number: 2015908225

CPSIA Code: PRT0715A
ISBN-13: 978-1-62086-915-4

Printed in the United States

MY MAMA LOVES ME

I'm Her Little Girl

Written by
Shanalee Sharboneau

Illustrated by
Israel Dilean

My mama loves me.

My mama sings to me.

My mama makes my dreams come true.

My mama wakes me.

My mama takes care of me.

My mama starts
my day with love.

My mama walks with me.

My mama talks with me.

My mama listens to my thoughts.

My mama stays with me.

My mama plays with me.

My mama loves me all life long.

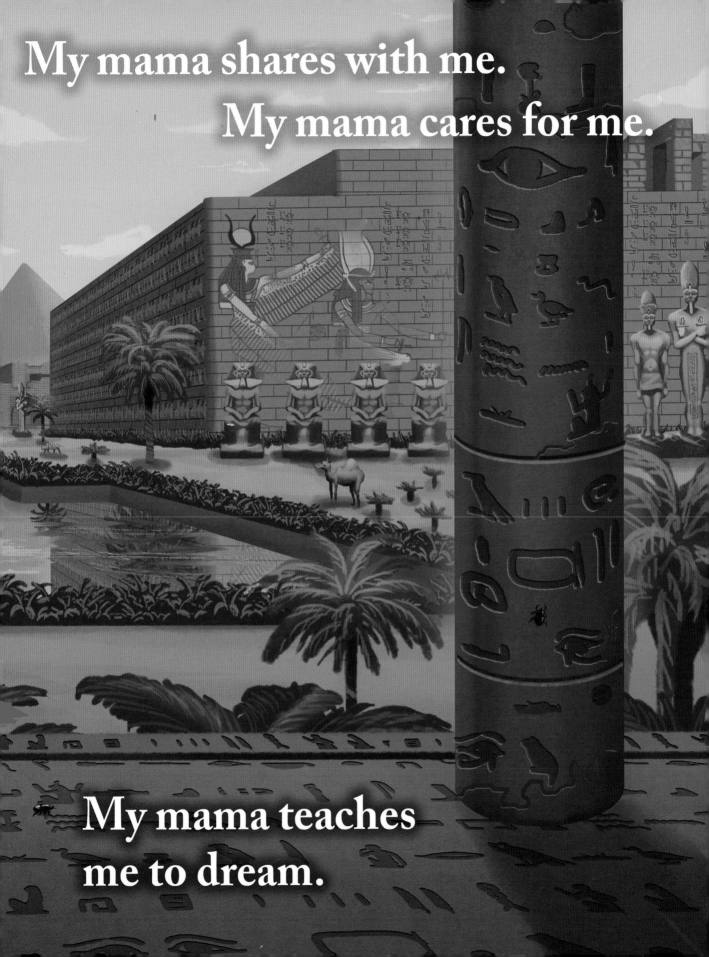

My mama shares with me.
My mama cares for me.

My mama teaches
me to dream.

My mama praises me.

My mama bathes me.

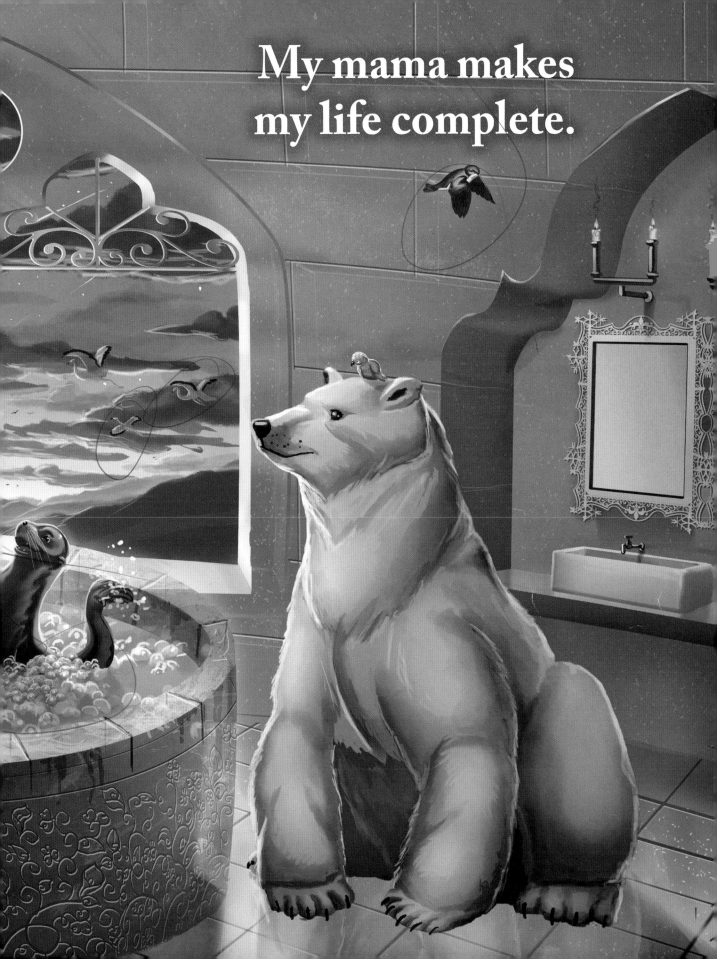

My mama makes
my life complete.

My mama kisses me.
My mama misses me.

My mama worries
all day long.

My mama teaches me.

My mama reaches for me.

My mama fills me up with hope.

My mama holds me.

My mama molds me.

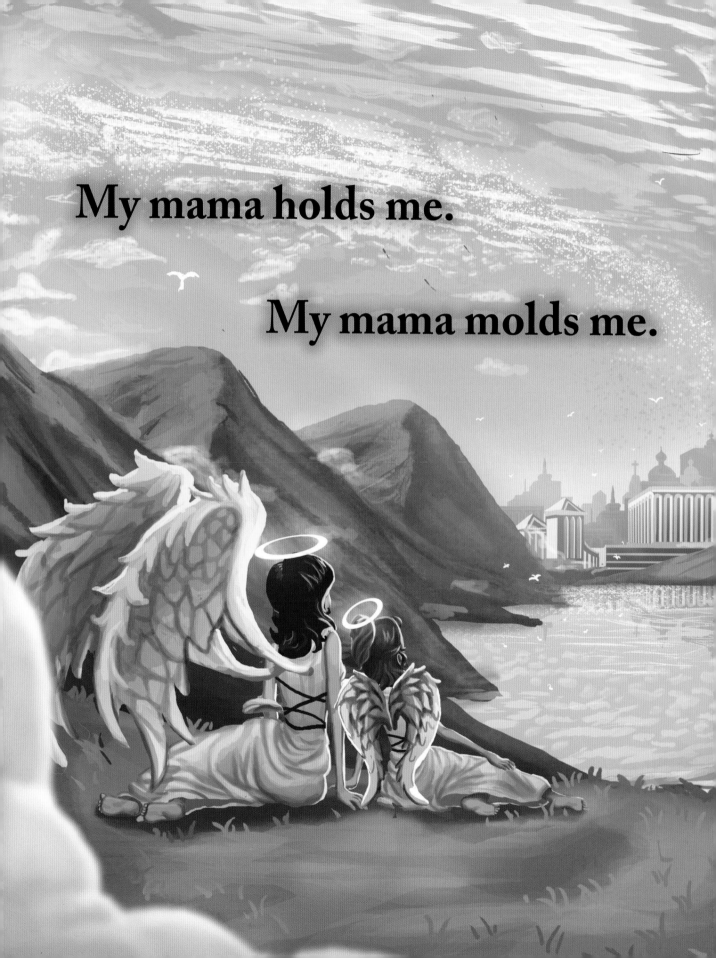

My mama folds my
hands in prayer.

My mama holds me
all night long.

My mama loves me.

My mama loves me.

My mama loves me
all life long.

Author Shanalee Sharboneau with her mother,
Cassaundra and son, Braydon

About the Author

Shanalee Sharboneau spent most of her life in Texas. With Irish immigrant grandparents, she grew up hearing tales of Vikings, castles, leprechauns, and banshees.

When Shanalee's son Braydon was born in 2010, he had severe reflux. She and her husband, Perry, spent the first six months with their son on a 24/7 vigilant watch to make sure his condition did not take him back to heaven.

Shanalee spent countless hours rocking her son day and night humming nursing tunes to calm him. None of them worked, until she began to hum a melody which later formed words. These words turned into lyrics, lyrics turned into verses, and the verses became the beautiful lullaby she sang to her newborn son entitled, "My Mama Loves Me".

After Braydon's reflux went away, Shanalee wrote down all the melodies to the lullaby so she would not forget the loving song she once sang to her infant son, over and over again, to calm him in his time of need.

This song was transformed into the book *My Mama Loves Me: I'm Her Little Boy*. *My Mama Loves Me: I'm Her Little Girl* is the second book in the *My Family Loves Me* series.

Upcoming titles

MY DADDY LOVES ME: *I'm His Little Boy*

MY DADDY LOVES ME: *I'm His Little Girl*

MY GRANDMA LOVES ME: *I'm Her Little Boy*

MY GRANDMA LOVES ME: *I'm Her Little Girl*

MY GRANDPA LOVES ME: *I'm His Little Boy*

MY GRANDPA LOVES ME: *I'm His Little Girl*

Check out *My Mama Loves Me: I'm Her Little Boy*, the first book in the *My Family Loves Me* series.

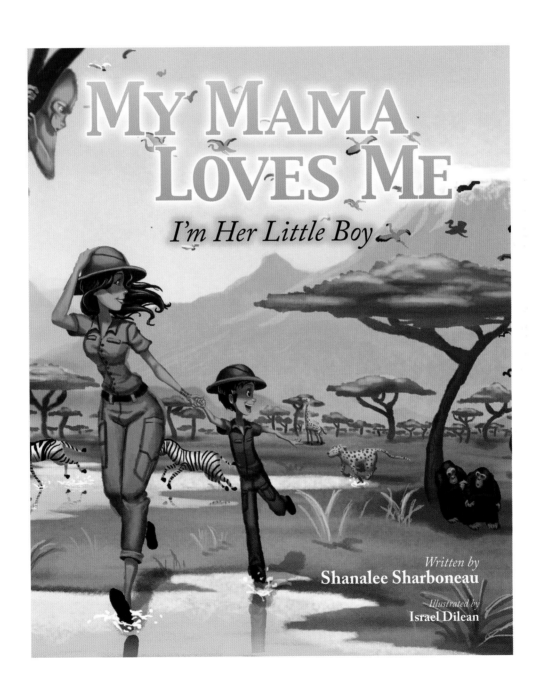